# Disney
# Olaf's
# FROZEN
# ADVENTURE

randomhousekids.com

ISBN 978-0-7364-3815-5

Printed in the United States of America
10 9 8 7 6 5 4 3 2 1

# DISNEP
# Olaf's
# FROZEN
# ADVENTURE

## The Deluxe Junior Novelization

Retold by Suzanne Francis

Random House 🏠 New York

# Chapter 1

Princess Anna gestured to a spot in the shade of a big twisted oak tree and smiled at her sister. "What do you think?" she asked.

Queen Elsa nodded. "Perfect," she replied. She helped Anna spread an oversized blanket onto the soft grass. Once it was stretched out nice and flat, the two collapsed on top.

"Oh, I love these sister picnics," said Anna, grinning. She sat up and peered into the picnic basket. "Mostly for the sandwiches," she added.

"They're definitely the best part." Elsa rolled

1

over and propped herself on her elbows.

Anna picked up a neatly wrapped sandwich and handed it to Elsa. "But being with you isn't so bad, either."

Elsa chuckled. "Thank you," she said. "You're pretty good company yourself."

At the beginning of the summer, the sisters had vowed to have a weekly picnic, and it had turned into a great little tradition. They were able to do two of their favorite things: spend time together and explore. Each week they'd hike, heading in whichever direction their feet chose to take them, until they found a beautiful spot. As autumn deepened, though, the growing chill made picnics outdoors more difficult.

After taking a few bites of her sandwich, Anna stretched out on the blanket and looked up at the last few leaves dangling from the giant oak, the sun sparkling around their curved edges. Two leaves fell as a breeze blew. Now only one remained, and Anna pointed it out to Elsa. The sisters lay side by side, admiring

the last clinging leaf for a moment before realizing what it actually meant.

"I can't believe it's almost winter," said Anna.

Elsa sighed in agreement. "I know," she said. "Fall went so fast."

It was strange to think about all that had changed in the past year. And not just for Anna and Elsa, but for everyone in Arendelle. The last time the cold had come was not in winter—it was when Elsa had caused a magical snowstorm! That was before she had learned to control her magical powers, when she and Anna had hardly spent any time together at all, and when Anna had nearly frozen to death. The cold would soon be back, but this time it would happen naturally.

Life was so much better now, and the sisters appreciated each other every single day.

Anna bolted upright and her eyes brightened. She had a great idea.

"Elsa!" she said, grabbing her sister's hand and pulling her to her feet. "I think this year we should celebrate winter!"

Elsa loved her sister's enthusiasm. "What do you have in mind?"

"I mean *really* celebrate," said Anna. "Do something big. Huge!"

"I like where you're going with this," said Elsa. "Something incredible. For the whole kingdom."

They racked their brains, searching for that big, huge, incredible thing that would ring in the winter. The holidays came to mind. It would be their first Christmas together!

"Well," said Elsa, "we could shine up the Yule Bell—try to make it look new."

When they were children, the bells in the tower were replaced with the giant Yule Bell during an annual ceremony. The sound of it ringing across Arendelle signaled the beginning of the holidays. But ever since their parents had died, the bell had been hidden away in storage.

"Ooh, that would be nice," said Anna. She imagined the beautiful, shiny bell hanging in the tower and all the people of Arendelle standing

below, smiling up at it, their hearts filling with joy. That gave her another idea. "How about a surprise celebration! After we ring the super-shiny Yule Bell, we'll surprise everyone with the biggest holiday party Arendelle has ever seen!"

"Yes!" Elsa said. The two wrapped up their picnic and started planning. They discussed countless ideas as they headed back to the castle.

When the sisters arrived home, they told Kai and Gerda, the family's longtime friends and faithful servants, about their plan.

"And it needs to be done in the next four weeks!" Anna exclaimed.

"What a lovely surprise!" said Gerda, beaming. "We will help you with everything you need."

"Of course we will," said Kai. He chuckled at the thought of their scheming to pull off such a surprise. "How very exciting!"

Soon the entire staff was on board, and they all began working together to plan for the celebration. The sisters also enlisted the help of

their best friends, Kristoff, Olaf, and Sven.

"But you can't tell anyone, Olaf," said Anna. She knelt to gaze into the little snowman's eyes as she tried to explain to him what a surprise party was. "It's a secret."

"Oh, I'm so excited!" said Olaf. "I won't say a word. Well, not until I can yell 'SURPRISE!'" He waved his twig arms around and bounced with delight. He was already counting the minutes until the day of the party, and he wondered how he could possibly stand the wait.

With no time to waste, everyone got to work. It all had to be perfect. Anna worked with Olina, the chef, to organize the menu, while Elsa spent time with some of the other staff members on the decorations. Each person in the castle had a job to do, and they were more than happy to help.

Kristoff volunteered to get the Yule Bell ready. "I'm sure I can shine it up," he said. "Olaf and Sven will help."

"Yes!" shouted Olaf, still hopping up and down, unable to contain his joy. "I have a job!"

As the weeks flew by, Elsa and Anna shared their accomplishments and asked for each other's opinions.

*"Kransekake!"* Anna shouted when she found Elsa in the hallway.

"I love *kransekake*," said Elsa, picturing the multilayered pastry. "Who doesn't?"

"Olina has Grandmother's recipe," said Anna. "We can make the biggest *kransekake* ever! Ours will be the tallest cake tower of all time."

"Yes!" said Elsa. "And we'll decorate it with something."

"Little flags," said Anna.

"Perfect," said Elsa. "So what do you think of this?" She held up a beautiful golden ornament. "For the pine trees in the ballroom. We can cover them with these and candles."

"Oh, that will look great," said Anna. "And how about some festive little brass bells? There's nothing like the sound of bells at Christmas."

"Definitely," said Elsa. "I have an idea for something to add to the menu: gingerbread!"

"Yum!" Anna said, her face lighting up. "We can make it look like our home! Instead of a gingerbread house—"

"A gingerbread castle!" the sisters said simultaneously. They smiled at each other and hurried off in opposite directions. They were thoroughly enjoying the planning process and were eager to share the fun with the townspeople.

While Anna and Elsa were busy inside, Kristoff was working in the courtyard. He had set up a large pulley to get the Yule Bell down from its storage place in the tower. He figured once he got the bell to the ground, he could store it in the stables. Then he could get started on shining it up.

"All right," said Kristoff as he secured Sven's harness to one end of the rope. "You wait here. When we get the bell hooked up, we'll come down and use the pulley to gently lower it to the ground."

This was the perfect time for Kristoff to practice his Sven mimicry. He imagined what

the reindeer would say, then said in a deep voice: *"Did you remember the carrots?"*

"Of course I did," said Kristoff in his normal voice. "I've got a whole bunch of fresh ones waiting for you in the stables."

*"You're the best,"* said Kristoff as Sven again. Sven played along, nuzzling his friend.

Kristoff patted the reindeer on the neck. "Oh, thanks, buddy."

"I'm here to help!" shouted Olaf as he hurried over to the tower. "Don't start without me!"

Kristoff greeted the little snowman, and the two started up the tower's steep, winding stairs. It took them quite a while to climb to the top, and when they got there, Olaf looked out and gasped at the sight below.

"Look at that!" he said. "We're as high as the sky!"

"It sure does feel like it," said Kristoff. He pushed open the heavy door to the storage space. "Dusty in here," he said. "Can you hold the door for me?"

"Yup," said Olaf. "I can do that." After all, his job was to help! He leaned against it.

Kristoff went inside and tapped on the side of the massive bell. It made a dull dinging noise. "Got it!"

"Wow," said Olaf. "What a beautiful sound."

Kristoff laughed. "Oh, just you wait," he said, checking to make sure the bell was sitting properly on the rolling cart. "Once it's hanging in the tower, you'll really hear what it's capable of." Kristoff thought back to the last time the bell had rung throughout the kingdom. "I've never heard a bell that sounds quite like the Yule Bell."

"I can't wait!" exclaimed Olaf. "I wish the celebration was today!"

As Kristoff began to push the cart, Olaf pressed his body against the door to keep it open. He scooted back as much as he could, because the bell was even bigger up close!

Kristoff paused as he nudged the cart through the doorway.

"We just have to secure it to the rope,

and then we'll head down to help Sven," he said, reminding Olaf of the plan.

But Olaf wasn't listening. He was far too interested in the giant bell. Mesmerized, he touched its smooth side. As he did, he let go of the door and—*WHAP!* It slammed shut, pushing the bell off the cart and down the stairs.

"Oh, no!" yelped Olaf.

He jumped onto the bell, trying to slow it down, but it was far too heavy. He gripped it tighter as it bounced down the stairway from the top of the tower.

Kristoff braced himself, expecting to hear a series of deafening rings, but there was only the sound of metal rolling against stone. Then he remembered that Sven was at the bottom of the stairs!

"Sven!" shouted Kristoff, rushing after Olaf and the runaway bell. "Watch out! It's coming down!"

The reindeer stepped aside as Olaf and the Yule Bell flew right out the tower door. The bell

rolled into the courtyard and continued a few feet before coming to a stop, gently swaying back and forth on an uneven spot in the cobblestone street. Olaf groaned as he slid off the bell.

"Why is the courtyard spinning?" the snowman asked. He stood up, dizzy from the ride. Kristoff ran to him to make sure he was okay. "Oh, hello. Hello." Olaf didn't understand why there were two Kristoffs all of a sudden. "I didn't know you had a twin brother. Nice to meet you."

"Sit down for a minute, Olaf," Kristoff said to his friend. "You'll be okay."

"Thanks," Olaf replied shakily.

Kristoff went over to the bell. After a quick inspection, he was relieved to see the metal hadn't cracked on its way down the stairs.

"It looks okay," he said. "But why didn't it ring?" He peered inside. Something was very wrong. "Oh, no." He stared at the hollow bell.

"What makes the bell ring?" asked Olaf. He stood beside Kristoff and followed his gaze.

He was pretty sure there was supposed to be something dangly inside.

Kristoff's shoulders slumped as he sighed dejectedly. "We have a Yule Bell that doesn't ring" he said. "Perfect."

# Chapter
# 2

**K**ristoff and Olaf searched the stairs of the tower and inside the storage space, but the Yule Bell's missing piece was nowhere to be found. They would have to find some way to replace it. Olaf had all kinds of ideas. He tried hanging various items inside the bell—his nose, a twig arm, and even one of his coals. Once Kristoff explained that the piece needed to be metal, Olaf tried using a spoon, but that didn't work, either.

Finally, the two headed over to the castle to share the news with Anna and Elsa. Kristoff

shuffled his feet as he and Olaf stood outside the
castle door, hesitating. He didn't want to let the
sisters down.

"I think I should probably do the talking,"
whispered Kristoff. "Okay?"

Olaf nodded in agreement. Kristoff put his
hands on the door, about to push it open, but
Anna came rushing out and nearly bumped into
him!

"Oh, hey there!" said Anna. "Wow. Just the
guys I wanted to see."

Kristoff smiled. "Oh, you were looking for
us? Ha, ha. Funny." He forced a nervous laugh.
"Because we were looking for you."

Anna smiled. "Let me go first," she said. She
had a surprise for them, and she couldn't keep it
in any longer. "Where's Sven?"

Eventually, they found Sven in the courtyard.
Anna asked Kristoff, Olaf, and Sven to close
their eyes.

"Okay, here we come," called Anna. "No
peeking!"

Elsa came into the courtyard. She and Anna were carrying large boxes. After a few moments, they shouted, "Surprise!"

Kristoff, Olaf, and Sven opened their eyes to see the sisters holding up clothing.

"For the holiday celebration!" Anna said proudly.

"We wanted to thank you for all your help with the planning," said Elsa.

"And commend your excellent secret-keeping skills," added Anna, with a wink at Olaf.

"This is for Sven," said Elsa, showing off a green velvet blanket embroidered with sparkling gold details. The reindeer clomped his hooves against the cobblestone and gave an approving snort.

"And this one is for you," said Anna, facing Kristoff. She revealed a beautiful suit—black pants, a blue coat, and a vest with shiny gold buttons. In her other hand was a new pair of shoes.

Kristoff was touched. He had never worn

anything so fancy before. "Wow," he said, examining the fine fabrics.

"And this is for you, Olaf," said Elsa. She held up a bright green bow tie. She was pretty sure Olaf would lose it, but Anna had said he would appreciate it anyway.

"I love it!" shouted Olaf. He leaned over to Kristoff and whispered, "What is that thing?"

Hearing Olaf's confusion, Elsa laughed. "It's a bow tie," she explained. "Something worn for special occasions." She secured it around Olaf's neck, checking the size. It fit!

"Thank you," he said. The edges of the tie tickled his neck, making him giggle.

Kristoff touched the shimmering buttons on his new vest. "These are great," he said sincerely.

The sisters smiled.

"I knew you'd like those," said Anna.

"I love them," he said, giving her a hug. "Thank you."

"What are you going to wear?" asked Olaf. "Maybe we can get you something special.

Matching bow ties, perhaps?"

Elsa laughed. "You're sweet, Olaf, but we were going to go out and get ours—"

Anna interrupted her. "Yoo-hoo!"

Elsa turned to Anna and was stunned to see her holding up two beautiful blue gowns.

"Surprise!" Anna said, grinning.

"Anna . . ." Elsa couldn't believe her sister had managed to surprise her! "They're gorgeous." She reached out and touched the lovely dark blue gown that she knew was meant for her. It was floor-length and elegant, with a white fur collar and a wispy, sheer cape. All along the edges of the material were delicate snowflakes.

"Yup. That one's yours. How'd you guess?" Anna teased. Then she wiggled the light blue gown. "And this one's mine." Anna's dress was bolder and more rustic, with big blue buttons and a mountain-goat detail across the bottom that reminded her of Arendelle's natural beauty. It even had a purple sash.

Elsa ran her fingers across the furry collar on

her dress. And the sheer cape practically floated across her hand.

"I can't believe you did this," she said. "I love it."

Anna smiled. "Do you like mine?" she asked, draping the gown against herself.

"They're both amazing," said Elsa. "Thank you so much."

"You're welcome," said Anna. Then she turned to Kristoff. "So you said you were looking for us? What was that about?"

"Oh, right," said Kristoff. "Nothing much. Just, um . . ." He cleared his throat. "There's a little problem with the bell."

"What? Repeat that?" asked Anna. She wasn't sure she'd heard him correctly.

"There is . . . a little problem . . . with the Yule Bell," said Olaf, slowly and loudly.

The sisters gasped.

"Oh no!" exclaimed Elsa. "What is it? The holidays can't happen without the Yule Bell."

Kristoff explained that the bell was missing

a piece, and then walked the sisters over to the stables. There was the bell, sitting on its side in a cushion of hay.

Anna elbowed Elsa. "I thought I remembered it being a lot . . ."

". . . shinier?" Elsa finished in a whisper. The bell looked dull and dark. But Kristoff's job was to polish it. Once he found the missing piece, at least.

"I'm sure we can fix it," said Kristoff as the sisters peered inside the huge bell. Knowing how important it was to the kingdom, he hoped he was right.

"It's missing the dangly metal thingy, right?" asked Anna.

Kristoff nodded. "Yup. We looked everywhere for it."

"It must have fallen off the last time the bell was moved," said Elsa, concerned.

"I tried to replace it, but it didn't sound very good," said Olaf.

"We need someone who can make a new one," said Kristoff. "And fast."

"A new dangly metal thingy," said Anna. She turned to Elsa. "Frederik."

"Frederik!" exclaimed Elsa in agreement.

The kingdom's most experienced blacksmith was just the person they needed to help figure out a solution. They sent a messenger to bring him to the bell that very day.

"Hmmm," said Frederik, drumming his fingers on his apron. He was a short, round man, and he looked even smaller next to the giant Yule Bell. He gazed inside. Then he circled around it, checking the metal from every angle. His wiry gray eyebrows moved toward his nose as he frowned, deep in thought. "So you need a new clapper."

"*That's* what it's called!" exclaimed Anna. "A lot catchier than 'dangly metal thingy.'"

Frederik laughed. "But not nearly as descriptive," he said kindly.

"Do you think you can fix it?" asked Elsa.

"Of course I can, Your Majesty," said Frederik. "But the holidays are right around the corner. I will have to work quickly." He explained a bit about the process. "Clappers are tricky. If they're too heavy, they crack the bell. If they're too light, they don't ring out. And if they're made of the wrong material or are the wrong shape, they go *blech* instead of *laaaaaa*!" He raised his arms and belted out a long operatic note. Then he knocked on the side of the bell with his knuckles. "We can do it."

"We need to have it in time for a special ceremony," Elsa said anxiously, being careful not to reveal too much about the surprise.

"Of course we do!" said Frederik. He smiled, and his cheeks popped out like two cherry blossoms in the spring. "I can't wait to hear the joyful sound of the Yule Bell again. I'll get to work right away." He said he would make the clapper in his shop, then return to attach it to the bell.

The sisters bid him farewell. They knew he could do it!

A few days later, the first snow came. Arendelle sparkled white in the crisp winter air. Everyone involved in planning the surprise party grew more excited each day. Elsa and Anna kept their minds off the Yule Bell as they focused on getting everything else ready.

Kristoff spent nearly all his time inside the stables, working on shining and refurbishing the Yule Bell, while Frederik did his best to make a new clapper. Every few days, he went to the stables to test out a design. He'd say "Too tinny" or "Too *blech*," then hurry back to his shop to continue his work.

The day before the ceremony, Elsa and Anna were going over their lists. It seemed everything was in order and ready to go . . . everything but the Yule Bell. When they'd spoken with him the day before, Frederik had said the clapper was almost ready. They couldn't help worrying. Would it be finished in time?

The day quickly slipped away. As the sun went down, they headed to the stables to check in with Kristoff. When they got there, they were

shocked to see how shiny the bell was.

"Wow!" said Anna. "It looks amazing!"

"Not bad, huh?" said Kristoff, giving the giant bell a final buffing with a rag.

"I feel like I can almost see myself in it!" added Olaf, squinting as he tried to make out his reflection in the surface of the bell.

"Let's just hope it can ring!" said Anna. "Have you seen—"

Before she could finish, there was a tapping noise from inside the bell. Kristoff smiled and stepped away, revealing Frederik in there!

Frederik chuckled when he saw the surprise on their faces. "All done." He stepped out of the bell and stood up tall. "Tomorrow we shall have a beautiful *laaaaaa,*" he sang in his best opera voice.

Anna ran up and hugged him. "Thank you! Thank you!"

"No need for thanks," Frederik said. "I did it for me as much as I did it for you and everyone else in the kingdom." He patted Anna on the

back. "We all need to hear the Yule Bell. Without its joyful ringing, there simply is no holiday in Arendelle."

Frederik smiled as he put on his coat and went back to the village. The group looked out the stable door and watched as the snow fell on the moonlit courtyard. Elsa and Anna sighed with relief.

"So I guess we're all ready for tomorrow," said Elsa.

"All ready," said Anna. "Now we just have to figure out how to fall asleep tonight."

They stood for another moment, appreciating the peaceful beauty of the courtyard at night and imagining it bustling with the energy of the holiday festivities to come.

# Chapter

# 3

Snow fell on Arendelle overnight, covering it like a thick layer of frosting on a gingerbread village. The next day, the streets buzzed with joyful cheer as people hurried about, finishing their last-minute shopping and exchanging friendly hellos. There was no denying it— Arendelle was bursting with a special holiday spirit.

Inside the castle, lovely smells filled the air as both savory and sweet holiday treats were being baked in the kitchen. It was all coming together.

Everyone continued to work hard. Servants set tables with colorful centerpieces and brought out trays of food.

Elsa and Anna had made sure that touches of holiday cheer graced nearly every corner of the castle. Pine wreaths dotted with little flowers and bright red velvet ribbons tied into bows hung throughout the hallways. Thick red ribbons were wrapped around the castle's columns, making them look like giant peppermint sticks. Towering evergreen trees stood tall in every room. They had been trimmed with shimmering gold ornaments, bells, and candles, just like the sisters had wanted.

Kai happily carried a basket of ornaments toward one of the half-decorated trees in the library. Like everyone else who was in on the surprise, he was thrilled that the day of the celebration had arrived. As he picked up an ornament and carefully hung it from one of the branches, Olaf's face popped out, startling him.

"SURPRISE!" shouted the little snowman,

peering through the pine needles.

Kai gasped and nearly dropped his basket! When he realized it was just Olaf, he chuckled. "Not yet," he said.

Olaf was having an extremely difficult time containing his excitement. He didn't know if he would be able to wait another minute!

Half a dozen servants made their way toward the dining room carrying tall stacks of pretty holiday dishes. They marched through a hallway lined with shiny suits of armor propped up as knights standing at attention. Suddenly, one of the masks popped open and Olaf peeked out!

"Surprise!" he cried.

The startled servants screeched as they clutched the swaying dishes, protecting them from crashing to the floor. Relieved it was the snowman, the servants sighed.

"Not yet, Olaf," they sang.

In the study, a fire warmed the room, throwing a pleasing glow onto a decorated pine tree. A mound of brightly wrapped gifts sat beside the tree. Nuf, another servant, entered the

room carrying an oddly shaped gift. As he added it to the pile, Olaf jumped out from behind him and shouted, "SURPRISE!"

The shock sent Nuf toppling into the presents, and they scattered and rolled around the room. Exasperated, he said, "Not yet, Olaf!"

Anna, already dressed in her beautiful blue holiday gown, slowly opened the door to the quiet, decorated ballroom to get a look inside. The room had been completely transformed. Lovely linens, candles, and centerpieces graced each table. The banisters on either side of the grand staircase had been wrapped with pine garland. Red ribbons and wreaths were scattered throughout the room, and candles had been placed in all the wall sconces, creating an elegant atmosphere. There were trees trimmed with gold, and some of the food had been set out on long tables. The ballroom looked even better than she and Elsa had imagined!

"Whoa," she said, admiring it all. Then she noticed the towering *kransekake* sitting on one of the tables. The sweet rings of cake were stacked

high and decorated with little blue flags, just like she and Elsa had planned.

"Hello," Anna said to the sweet treat. Surely no one would mind if she sneaked a teeny, tiny taste.

Suddenly, Olaf burst from the cake. "SURPRISE!" he shouted. When he tumbled out, his parts separated along with the rings of the *kransekake*. Little blue flags fluttered everywhere.

Olaf's head flew high up into the air, and Anna caught it in her arms. A blue flag stuck out of his snowy skull. He grinned up at her.

"Olaf, not yet!" said Anna with a giggle. She understood why he was so excited. She felt the same way!

Elsa descended the staircase sprinkling icy magic along the garland, making it glitter and sparkle. Her gown looked gorgeous, and its sheer cape sparkled with magic—her own special touch to Anna's gift. The dress's long train dragged behind her and gracefully swept down the staircase as she walked.

"Anna's right," she said. "Our surprise holiday party doesn't start until *after* the Yule Bell rings!" She reminded Olaf to be patient.

"Ah," he sighed, his head still in Anna's arms. "Sorry, the suspense is tearing me apart!" The different sections of his body shook off the cake rings and pieced themselves back together. Anna put his head back on. "Thank you!"

"Olaf, I'm eager, too," said Anna. "This is Arendelle's first Christmas in forever!"

Elsa took the tiny blue flag from Olaf's head. "The first of many to come," she said with a smile.

Just then, something drew Anna's attention. She looked outside. "Elsa, look!" she shouted, rushing to the window. "They're arriving!"

Elsa ran over. The sight of the townspeople below filled the sisters' hearts with joy.

# Chapter
## 4

Everyone streamed over the cobblestones, dressed in their best holiday clothes and looking cheerful and vibrant. Anna, Elsa, and Olaf watched for a moment, delighted to see the people admiring the festive decorations. Elsa and Anna had left out no decorating detail. They had made sure the courtyard was as magical as the castle. Pine trees covered in snow dotted the area and, thanks to Elsa's magic, towering ice sculptures sprouted from the fountains that flanked the castle.

The townspeople were amazed by the outside decorations, but Elsa, Anna, and Olaf couldn't wait until they saw what was waiting for them inside. The party was bound to be the best surprise Arendelle had ever seen. Knowing the wait was nearly over made them feel they might burst!

Anna knew the townspeople would love it all as much as she and Elsa did. She checked again to make sure everything was perfect. The last trays of food were in place. She examined one of the little centerpieces Elsa had shown her, a miniature tower surrounded by candles and tiny bells. Leaning in, she couldn't help ringing a few just for fun. The tinkling sound sent a rush of joy through her.

Elsa also gave everything one last glance before they went down to greet the guests. She and Anna looked festive in their new holiday gowns, and Anna had braided some red berries and pine into her hair.

"You both look so beautiful!" said Olaf.

Elsa noticed that Olaf wasn't wearing his green bow tie.

"I used it to shine up the Yule Bell," Olaf admitted. "It did a really good job! But it got dirty."

Elsa glanced around the room, looking for something special to give him. Her eyes landed on the perfect thing: a little red petal from a flower on one of the hanging wreaths! She plucked it off and placed it on Olaf, beneath his chin, and it looked just like a bow tie. Olaf instantly felt fancier. He thanked Elsa for helping him look his best.

Anna and Elsa smiled at each other. There was only one last thing to do! As they passed the gingerbread castle, which matched their home exactly, Anna sprinkled powdered sugar on top. It looked like the snow that had blanketed Arendelle overnight. Then Elsa pushed open the miniature front gates.

It was time!

Anna, Elsa, and Olaf rushed into the

courtyard, waving at the townspeople and welcoming them. They all responded happily.

A group of people ringing handbells strode through the center of the courtyard. Behind them, Kristoff walked beside Sven, who proudly pulled a cart that carried the giant, shiny Yule Bell. Kristoff and Sven looked great in the holiday clothes Anna and Elsa had given them.

Olaf gasped when he saw his friends enter the courtyard.

"Hey, it's Kristoff and Sven!" he said breathlessly, his body quivering. "AND THE YULE BELL!" He paused, then chuckled, looking at the sisters. "Why am I so excited about that?"

"Olaf, remember: the Yule Bell signals the start of the holidays in Arendelle," said Elsa.

"Ooohh," replied Olaf. In his excitement, he had completely forgotten that very important detail.

Everyone oohed and aahed as the bell was pulled into the center of the courtyard. Wheeling

out the old bell was clearly a tradition that the whole kingdom revered and had missed. The townspeople chattered about how beautifully shined and buffed the bell looked. Frederik beamed, glad the bell was working again.

Kristoff raced to the top of the tower. The bells that normally hung there had been moved to the storage area, making room for the majestic Yule Bell. Down below, Frederik and a group of other townspeople huddled around, ready to help. When Kristoff was ready, he gave the signal. Then they all worked together to hoist the bell high over the courtyard.

From the tower, Kristoff helped guide it up. Once it was securely in place at the center of the tower, he dropped the rope down to Anna and Elsa. They stood on a platform in front of the townspeople. Everyone was eagerly waiting for the clock to strike twelve!

Olaf fidgeted with the rope from below as he watched along with the townspeople. When the hands of the clock ticked to noon, Anna, Elsa,

and Olaf pulled on the rope. The heavy bell swung back and forth—and rang triumphantly! The deep, rich, beautiful sound carried across the kingdom. Anna and Elsa remembered Frederik singing *"Laaaaaa!"* in his dramatic opera voice and they smiled.

Elsa held her arms out to the people and shouted, "Let the holidays begin!"

The crowd roared with cheers and applause. Anna leaned over to Olaf.

"Okay, NOW!" she said as they opened the castle doors.

Finally allowed to share the secret, Olaf shouted, "SURPRISE!" as loudly as he could.

But when Anna turned around, everyone was walking away from the castle. Anna and Elsa stood there for a moment, bewildered. Why weren't the townspeople happily surprised and ready to celebrate with them? Why were they leaving? And where were they going?

"Uh-oh," said Olaf, just as perplexed and disappointed as the sisters.

Anna rushed off the steps of the castle. She could hear the townspeople talking about how beautiful the ceremony was and how much they loved the Yule Bell as they left.

She shouted, "Wait! Wait! Hold on! Hold on!" as she hurried over, trying to catch up. She saw a grandmother holding her little granddaughter's hand and shifted her panicked voice to a casual one.

"Going so soon?" Anna asked.

The grandmother turned to her and smiled kindly. "The Yule Bell rang," she said. "I must get home to my family's holiday tradition: rolling the *lefse*!" She pulled her granddaughter along as they headed away.

Anna understood the tradition: the flat-bread was delicious! And maybe the grandmother and her family hadn't planned on spending the evening in the castle. That was all right—surely someone else could stay.

Anna looked at a couple hurrying out.

"We put out porridge for our *tomte*!" the man

explained. *Tomte* were little elves that were said to keep the farms safe.

A pair of twin sisters rushed by. "We're baking traditional *bordstabelbakkels*!" they said cheerfully. Anna loved the cookies, but she wished the sisters didn't have to make them now.

Olaf wanted to share something, too. "And I'm going to fillet the *krumsalakringlekakke*," he said. He turned to Anna. "That's a thing, right?"

Anna shook her head. Her heart sank to her feet as she watched the people go. None of them had planned on celebrating at the castle. Even Kristoff had disappeared somewhere. They were all on their way home to do the various things they did every year. Anna and Elsa's surprise had been too much of a surprise.

As the townspeople continued to announce a variety of family traditions, Elsa came down to the courtyard, too. She approached a couple that was ambling out arm in arm. She smiled.

"Oh, Mr. and Mrs. Olsen," she said, "you're welcome to join us in the castle if you'd like."

"Thank you, Your Majesty," said Mr. Olsen, resting his cane against the cobblestone. "But Olga and I should be getting home to knit socks for our grandchildren."

"It's our tradition," added Olga.

"Yes, and we wouldn't want to intrude on *your* family traditions," said Mr. Olsen. The couple smiled and continued on their way.

Anna and Elsa stood still as statues, listening to the hollow echo of footsteps as the courtyard emptied. They stared at the space around them, disappointed. It certainly was not the sight they had expected to see after the ceremony. Where was the joyous surprise celebration they'd planned for? Why did it seem that everyone but them had something else to do?

They thought about Mr. Olsen's words. *"We wouldn't want to intrude on* your *family traditions."* Everyone's traditions seemed so wonderful. The sisters couldn't help feeling they were the only two in the entire kingdom who were missing something.

Olaf brightened. "Oh, so the surprise is that everyone left?"

Anna and Elsa sighed, too sad to respond. Then they heard the faint sound of music coming from the courtyard entrance.

# Chapter 5

Kristoff sauntered into the courtyard, playing his lute. He was wearing a moss cape with a big collar made of bright green fern fronds that flapped in the breeze. He knew how disappointed the sisters were after they'd looked forward to celebrating with everyone, and he was confident that he could make them feel better.

"Hey," he said, casually strumming a few upbeat chords. "I say it's their loss! Who needs a *big* party anyway?"

"Kristoff?" said Anna, surprised to see him

in the strange costume. She wondered what he was up to.

"I've got just the thing to cheer you up: my favorite traditional troll tradition." He leaned into Anna. "Care to join in?"

"Uh, *yeah*!" said Anna. She was excited at the prospect of sharing in a holiday tradition.

"Okay, it starts with a gathering song," said Kristoff. " 'The Ballad of Flemmingrad.' " He struck a few chords dramatically.

Olaf squealed. "I LOVE BALLADS!" He bounced up and down, clapping his hands.

Kristoff continued to play, and he danced around the courtyard as he sang. Sven trotted to the beat of the music, pulling a small wooden wagon behind him, on which something sat mysteriously covered by a dark cloak.

The sisters enjoyed the music, and Olaf joined in. He used a twig arm as a flute to accompany Kristoff's jolly tune.

"Tempo!" shouted Olaf, trying to keep the beat moving.

Kristoff carried on his serenade. The sisters were charmed by the sweet tune at first, but then the song started to get a little weird when the lyrics mentioned stuffing grass up a troll's nose. Sven held a clump of grass in his teeth and dropped it into Elsa's hands. He was asking her to participate.

Then Sven grabbed the cloak on the wagon with his teeth and yanked it off with a flourish—to reveal a sculpture of Flemmy the fungus troll. It was an absolutely disgusting-looking creation made of mud, fungus, rocks, and grass. Branches with dead brown leaves dangling from them stuck out on either side of the troll. Olaf gasped with glee and put his hands over his mouth.

Anna and Elsa were stunned. They had heard the legend of Flemmy, the hero troll who had saved all trollkind, but they had no idea what he would look like in statue form!

"Whoa, gross," said Anna.

As Kristoff finished singing, one of Flemmy's stone eyes fell off. Olaf quickly picked it up and

stuffed it back on his mushy mud face.

At the end of the song, Kristoff smiled. "Now you lick his forehead and make a wish." He bent and gave the troll sculpture a big lick. When he turned to Anna and Elsa, he had mud and moss all over his mouth and chin. "Who's next?" he asked, grinning widely.

The sisters were horrified. Anna stuck an elbow out and nudged Elsa's arm.

"Elsa!" she said. "You're up."

"Come on," urged Kristoff. "Tastes like lichen."

Elsa gagged at the thought of putting her mouth on the sticky mound of mud and moss.

Olaf leaned over to Anna and whispered, "You're a princess; you don't have to settle."

Anna and Elsa watched Flemmy drip and ooze onto the courtyard. They tried to figure out a way to respond without hurting Kristoff's feelings. His tradition was special, but it was *his*—not theirs.

"Okay, not so much a royal activity,"

Kristoff said, letting them off the hook. Sven gave Kristoff's face a big lick, cleaning off the mud and grass. "I get it. But wait until you taste my traditional Flemmy Stew!" He plucked a mushroom off Flemmy and threw it into an oversized pot. Sven jumped into the air and excitedly spun in a circle. "It may smell like wet fur, but it's a real crowd-pleaser!"

Sven danced on his hooves, nudging the pot with his nose. The stew was his favorite part of the holidays! Kristoff and Sven, pulling Flemmy on the wagon, trudged out of the courtyard to start cooking.

"Oh, thanks—we're good!" Anna called after him, not at all interested in the stew tradition, either.

"Big breakfast," Elsa added, patting her stomach as if she were far too full to eat even a tiny bite.

Excited all over again, Olaf took Anna's and Elsa's hands and pulled them out of the courtyard.

"Oooohh, I can't wait!" he said as they entered the castle.

Elsa looked at the little snowman, confused by his enthusiasm. "For what, Olaf?"

"For *your* family tradition!" said Olaf. "What is it? Tell me! Tell me! Tell me!" He bounced up and down.

Anna and Elsa looked at each other, both at a loss. They wished they had something to share with him, but they couldn't think of anything their family had done every year.

"Do we have any traditions, Elsa?" Anna asked. "Do you remember?" She gazed at her big sister with eyes full of hope. She thought maybe there was something. Maybe her poor memory was just blocking it out.

"Well, I remember . . ." Elsa's voice trailed off as she looked up at the old family portrait hanging on the wall. Her father stood beside her, and their mother sat holding baby Anna on her lap. Elsa stared at the image of the young family as she tried to recall what the

holidays were like for them back then.

She went to the window and tried to find the memories of holidays past playing out in the courtyard below. Then she could see her younger self, along with Anna and their parents, waving to the crowd that had gathered there, just like they had earlier that day. She saw the Yule Bell as it was brought in, and could picture it being raised up into the tower. Then she, her parents, and Anna had pulled the rope to ring in the holiday. The family smiled joyously as the bell rang out across the kingdom.

Elsa remembered hearing the sound of the bell and how it had made her feel. It was wonderful to be surrounded by such warm holiday joy and cheer. She recalled feeling happy and proud as she and her family celebrated the start of the season.

A small wrinkle formed above Anna's eyes as she frowned, confused. "But the Yule Bell was for the whole kingdom," she said. "What about us?"

"After the gates were closed, we were never together," said Elsa, still staring out the window, her eyes full of sorrow. Her gaze fell to the floor as she sighed and turned away. Deep down, Elsa knew she shouldn't blame herself for the way the magical powers she was born with had interfered with their childhood, but she often did. She couldn't help thinking her family *would* have had some lovely annual family tradition, like everyone else in the kingdom, if it hadn't been for her.

"Elsa?" Anna said, watching her sister walk across the floor.

"I'm sorry, Anna," Elsa said. "It's my fault we don't have a tradition." She hurried out of the ballroom.

"Wait, Elsa!" said Anna, rushing after her. But by the time she got to the doorway, Elsa was gone.

Olaf watched as Anna paused at the closed door separating her from her sister and put her hands against it. It was a familiar scene from

their childhood, and Anna felt just as terrible as she had all those years before. She slumped her shoulders and walked out of the room, feeling empty and alone.

Olaf lowered his head. He hated seeing Elsa and Anna unhappy, and wished he could do something to help. He would give anything to fix it, if he only knew how. The sisters had worked so hard for so long to give everyone a holiday surprise. He couldn't bear to think of them being alone and sad.

Suddenly, a smile flashed across his face. Armed with an idea, he dashed from the room.

# Chapter
# 6

Olaf rushed out of the castle and made his way to the stables. Sven was relaxing inside, slowly munching on some fresh hay.

"Sven!" hissed Olaf. "Anna and Elsa don't have a family tradition."

The reindeer groaned and hung his head.

"I know it's sad," Olaf said. "But I have a solution!"

Sven perked up. He lifted his head and waited to hear Olaf's idea.

"We'll go and find the best traditions Anna

and Elsa have ever seen. We'll bring items back
to the castle so they can decide what they'd like
to do themselves! Are you with me?" Olaf held
out a twig arm, and Sven grunted as he gave him
a high five—knocking the arm clear off Olaf's
body and sending it into the courtyard.

"Ow!" Olaf winced in pain but continued
to smile.

The friends acted swiftly. First, they prepared
Kristoff's sleigh. Then they got Sven ready and
hitched him up to it. In no time at all, Olaf was
sitting in the driver's seat, holding the reins,
as Sven pulled the sleigh out of the stables and
into the courtyard.

"Let's go find their tradition!" Olaf cheered.
With the wind rushing past, Olaf felt exhilarated
and full of hope as they raced across the courtyard
and through the castle gates.

They went into town and stopped in front
of the first home they saw. Olaf went up to the
door. He knocked and knocked until he heard a
woman call in a singsong voice, "Coming!"

Finally, Frigga, a short woman with a kind face, came with her son, Ben. Olaf stood there grinning.

"Good afternoon!" he said. "I am Olaf—"

"Hey, Olaf!" said Ben, enthusiastically shaking Olaf's twig arm.

"Please let me finish," said Olaf firmly. Then he returned to his friendly voice. "—and I like warm hugs." Olaf turned to gesture to Sven, still hitched to Kristoff's sleigh. "This is my associate, Sven." The reindeer lifted his head and grunted as if to say hello. Frigga and Ben smiled at them.

"We're going door-to-door looking for family traditions," continued Olaf. "Tell us yours and we'll decide if it's special enough to take back to the castle."

"Oh, we make candy canes together!" Frigga said brightly. She handed Olaf a thick, shiny, red-and-white-striped piece of candy.

"Ohhhhh!" said Olaf, grabbing the sweet treat. He removed his carrot nose and pushed the candy cane in its place. His head instantly

popped up off his body and his eyes rolled around in his head. "Sugar rush!" He giggled.

Ben plucked the candy cane from Olaf's face and stuck it into the snowman's mouth. "You're supposed to *eat* it," he explained.

"Eat my new nose?" exclaimed Olaf. "Why would I do that?"

"Because it's that time of year!" said Ben, spinning around joyfully.

"Huh," said Olaf, popping his carrot nose back on. "It's *that time* of year!" he repeated. Olaf's smile widened as he realized just how special the holidays were. It felt great to be part of something that came once a year and meant so much to so many people. Feeling he could practically float with joy, Olaf thanked Ben and his mom for the candy cane and continued on his quest, heading to the next house and the next.

Olaf had a great time meeting everyone and hearing about all the different things they did for the holidays. He used a piece of parchment and a feather pen to catalog the great variety of

family traditions that were taking place across the kingdom. All the families were more than happy to talk with him. They were proud of their customs, and honored to give a sample to the queen and princess. Olaf piled the items in the sleigh to take back to Anna and Elsa.

One family liked to hang boughs of holly over all the doorways in their home. Olaf smiled as he watched their little dog trot up holding some of the long garland, helping them decorate.

Another tradition was baking a giant cookie in the shape of Arendelle. The family worked together to pull the enormous cookie out of the wood-burning oven and show it to Olaf. It smelled and looked delicious. The kids wore colorful paper hats and eyed the cookie hungrily. Olaf loved how warm, cozy, and happy it was in their little home.

On one street, Olaf found a group of neighbors singing holiday songs at every house. The singers wore matching shiny purple costumes, and they sang dramatically for anyone who would listen.

The group had even coordinated some dance moves. Olaf danced with them!

One family demonstrated how they hung stockings over an open fire. Olaf watched the fabric sway above the crackling flames.

"That seems safe," said Olaf, smiling awkwardly.

He thanked each family for sharing their special traditions. He was taking notes diligently. He couldn't wait to show everything to Elsa and Anna!

"We better get a move on if we're going to hit every house in the kingdom!" said Olaf. Sven nodded and took off toward the next street.

They continued on from house to house, finding new and different traditions and putting more and more items into their sleigh. It was filling up quickly!

One family celebrated Hanukkah with a spinning top called a dreidel. The children huddled around, taking turns playing with it. They also had a special candle lamp called a

menorah that they would light for eight nights in a row.

Another group danced in the snow wearing evergreen garland necklaces and chandeliers of lit candles on their heads. Olaf thought it was all so cheerful and festive. He couldn't possibly choose a favorite!

Another family's tradition was making fruitcake for their friends. They gave one of the cakes to Olaf and he gobbled down the entire thing in one gulp. It fell out of him and landed with a thud.

"That went right through me," he said, laughing. He picked the fruitcake up and tossed it into the sleigh.

At yet another house, the family explained that they'd bought presents for each other and hidden them. A little girl showed Olaf the mountain of gifts she'd put under her bed. There were so many that they lifted her bed off the floor! Her "secret" hiding place was not very secret at all.

One family explained how every year they would wait for a chubby man to slide down their chimney and bring them presents.

Olaf jotted this down. "Breaking and entering: okay on Christmas," Olaf noted cheerfully.

Everyone Olaf encountered was so happy and jolly, he couldn't help feeling the spirit of the holiday. Some townspeople played instruments and danced in the snow. Unable to pass them by, Olaf stopped to dance with them. A woman swung him around and around until he flew right off his twig arms! He landed in a windmill and spun around until he was flung back to the snowy ground. The woman hurried over, stuck his arms back on his body, and gave him a clarinet. He attempted to play it as everyone enjoyed the big dance party.

As Olaf knocked on more doors, he couldn't believe the number of new and interesting traditions there were. One family's tradition was knitting scarves, sweaters, and mittens. Just next door, their neighbor knitted pajamas

for her kittens every year. Kittens purred and peered around every inch of her house, wearing matching pajamas!

Soon a heaping mound of items representing all the traditions was piled high in Kristoff's sleigh. There was everything from mistletoe, garland, and sprigs of holly to candles, musical instruments, and figurines. The sleigh was packed! Olaf had collected something from each and every house—except one.

"One more house, Sven!" exclaimed Olaf, clambering onto the seat. "Something tells me this will be the best tradition yet."

He held the reins tight, and Sven led the way out of town, up toward the mountains.

# Chapter
## 7

The door opened. Oaken, the owner of Wandering Oaken's Trading Post and Sauna, stood tall, filling the doorframe. He looked down at the little snowman and smiled, immediately recognizing him.

"Hoo, hoo!" said Oaken in a friendly voice.

"Helloooo!" said Olaf, mimicking Oaken's singsong tone. "And what does *your* family do this time of year?"

"Ooohh!" said Oaken excitedly, pressing his index fingers together. He couldn't wait to show

It's Arendelle's first holiday with the gates open!
ELSA and ANNA decide to throw a surprise party.

OLAF helps the
sisters ring the
YULE BELL!

But when all the villagers leave to celebrate their **OWN TRADITIONS**, there is no one left at the party.

Even **KRISTOFF** has troll traditions.

Anna and Elsa don't remember having **ANY** traditions of their own.

### OLAF HAS AN IDEA!
He and Sven search the village to find the very best traditions to share with Anna and Elsa.

They find
**CANDY CANES** and
**FRUITCAKE**—and
even get a **SAUNA**
from Oaken.

But the
sauna lights
the sleigh
on **FIRE**!

The sleigh tumbles
**OFF THE CLIFF**,
and Olaf and Sven
are separated.

Meanwhile, Elsa and Anna search their attic for **TRADITIONS**.

They
find an
**OLD BOX**.

Sven returns and tells Kristoff and the sisters
that Olaf is **LOST IN THE WOODS**!

Anna and Elsa
gather the
**VILLAGERS**
to search for
the snowman.
They finally
find him.

To cheer Olaf up, Anna and
Elsa show him the old box.
It's **FULL** of drawings
and figures of him!

**OLAF** has always been
their tradition.

Anna and Elsa share a hug with
the **BEST TRADITION** of all!

Olaf his family's holiday tradition.

Moments later, Olaf and Oaken joined the entire Oaken family, cousins and all, inside a huge sauna. They were playing music, chatting, eating, and drinking—as if they were in someone's living room. Only instead of wearing fancy holiday dresses and suits or pajamas, they were all wearing bathing suits and towels!

The sauna was decorated with all the festive touches of a holiday party—there were even piles of wrapped gifts under several Christmas trees! Olaf was thrilled to be there, not only because he was enjoying the celebration, but also because it was his first time in a sauna. He had always wondered what it was like, and just as he had expected, it was toasty.

Oaken sat beside Olaf wearing nothing but a tiny towel.

"Enjoying the Christmas sweats, inquisitive magic snowman?" he asked.

Olaf, who was wearing his own little towel, was happy as can be. As he began to melt

from the intense heat, he replied, "Oh, yeah. Nothing like taking your coals off once in a while, you know what I mean? My troubles are just melting away."

Oaken nodded. He calmly pushed a wooden bucket under Olaf, catching the liquid snowman as he melted right off the bench. Then Oaken opened the door.

"In retrospect," he said, "the holiday sweats are for those not made of snow." He tossed out the melted Olaf, and as the carrot, twigs, and water hit the chilly air, they instantly froze together. Olaf reformed, now a solid piece of misshapen ice.

Sven tapped the translucent ice with his hoof, shattering it. Suddenly, Olaf was back to normal! He shook, and dozens of tiny ice chips flew off his body.

"Ohhhh, I feel so refreshed!" he exclaimed. He looked at his reflection in a big, shiny tuba sitting on top of the sleigh. "Am I glowing?"

*THUMP!* Oaken loaded a small sauna onto

the very top of the sleigh. "Here's a sauna for your friends," he said.

"Thank you, Mr. Wandering Oaken!" said Olaf gratefully. "Oh, one last thing. Would it be possible to get one of those awkwardly revealing yet tastefully traditional towels your family is so fond of wearing?"

"Take mine! Yah?" said Oaken, whipping off his towel and flinging it at Olaf's head.

"Ooohh, still warm!" said Olaf, enjoying the feel of the steamy towel on his face.

Olaf tied the towel around his middle and hopped onto the sleigh. It looked fantastic, fully loaded with holiday traditions. He grinned at Sven, knowing they had succeeded in their quest. They were ready to head back to the castle and share their finds with Anna and Elsa. He couldn't wait to see which tradition they chose!

Olaf climbed back into the driver's seat and

grabbed the reins. A squirrel scurried across a snow-covered tree branch and watched Olaf and Sven start off down the mountain. The traditions were piled so high, the sleigh teetered back and forth. The sauna, perched at the very top, swayed precariously. Olaf ignored it and began to sing.

The squirrel's bushy tail twitched as it watched Olaf. Feeling on top of the world, Olaf playfully ripped the towel from around his waist and swung it around, causing the sauna door to open. A single hot coal tumbled out.

When Olaf saw it, he quickly snatched it up and threw it out of the sleigh. "Crisis averted!" he cheered, pleased with himself. Then he continued with his happy song and dance.

The coal soared through the air and knocked the squirrel square in the head, then ricocheted back onto the sleigh! It rolled into some little straw goat ornaments and instantly sparked a flame. Olaf didn't notice.

As the flames spread, the sleigh broke away from the reindeer—except for one strap. The

sleigh gathered speed down the mountain, gradually overtaking Sven. Olaf, sitting atop the traditions that had not yet caught fire, zoomed past the sprinting reindeer.

"Oh, look!" he exclaimed. "Another reindeer!" He waved. "Hi!"

The fire crackled and roared, losing chunks of debris to one side, then the other. Olaf still didn't notice. "Wow, we're making really good time."

Sven dug his heels into the mountainside, trying to stop the sleigh. But the momentum was too much. At the edge of a cliff, *CRACK!* The sleigh snapped apart and launched into the air. The single strap connecting Sven to the sleigh broke, and the reindeer skidded to a halt.

The sleigh flew high over the cliff, sending the holiday items tumbling into a gorge. Olaf was catapulted across the divide, where he landed safely in the snow.

Olaf looked down over the edge, shocked and confused, watching as the sleigh fell.

"Hey, the fire's out!" he called over to Sven.

Then he and Sven watched, horrified, as the sleigh hit the bottom of the canyon. There was a moment of silence just before they heard a deafening boom as Kristoff's sleigh exploded in a great big raging ball of fire.

Olaf and Sven stared as the flames died down, revealing the burnt wreckage below. Black smoke billowed up between the canyon walls.

"Oh, darn it," said Olaf. The tradition items were gone.

# Chapter

## 8

**B**ack at the castle, Elsa was pacing around her
bedroom, feeling awful. She knew she shouldn't
have run out on her sister the way she had. The
fact that she had left her on the other side of a
closed door made her feel even worse. How could
she have stirred up those terrible old memories of
shutting Anna out? She had promised herself a
long time ago that she wouldn't do that to her
sister again. And yet here she was, locked away
in her bedroom after leaving Anna all alone.

She knew what she had to do to fix it. She

headed down the hallway to apologize.

Elsa stood for a moment in front of Anna's bedroom door and took a deep breath, collecting herself before turning the knob.

"Anna, I owe you an apology for earlier," she said, slowly opening the door. She peered inside but didn't see her sister anywhere. The room was empty. "Anna?"

*CRASH! THUMP!* A loud noise boomed from above. Elsa looked at the ceiling. *The attic,* she thought.

Elsa left the empty bedroom and made her way to the top of the castle. She pushed open a creaky hatch and climbed into the dark attic. Flickers of dust danced in the light of her lantern. It was quiet and creepy up there, and she spotted the outlines of boxes and furniture covered with tarps scattered throughout the space. She could also make out some cobwebs draped across the corners between some of the wooden beams.

*Thump! Clunk!* She heard the noise again, and as her heart rate increased, she shone her lantern

around the darkness, looking for the source. Finally, her light landed on a rustling shape in the corner.

Elsa gasped as Anna popped out of a big old trunk, wearing a goofy grin and some random accessories.

"Hi, Elsa!" she said, beaming.

"Anna? What are you doing up here?" asked Elsa, relieved.

"Looking for traditions," Anna said, slipping out of the trunk.

"And what are you wearing?" asked Elsa, eyeing her sister's odd hat and cape.

"My old Viking helmet!" Anna said proudly. "And this is my sorceress cloak!" she said, turning to reveal a big velvet cloak with a stiff collar. Then she lifted her foot and wiggled it around, showing off a large, scaly green slipper. "Dragon feet!" She mimicked a roaring dragon. *"Rahhh!"* She giggled. "I found them in my trunk."

Anna had really enjoyed being up in the attic, surrounded by all the memories. She showed

Elsa some of the other things she had found: her first bicycle, her favorite books, and even some birthday cards from her parents. It was nice to think about some of the good things she had experienced as a young girl. She had also found marbles, pebbles, and pressed flowers that she couldn't quite remember saving. Elsa reminded her that as a child she'd liked to collect "treasures." They were sure that those items were part of Anna's prize collection.

Finally, Anna stepped out of her trunk and headed over to Elsa. She couldn't wait to see what memories her sister had stored in the attic.

"What's in your trunk?" she asked eagerly.

"Oh, mostly gloves," said Elsa with a shrug.

Anna carefully made her way to another corner of the attic to a trunk with Elsa's name painted on it.

"Right," she said, chuckling. "Rows and rows of satin gloves." She lifted the lid and immediately stopped laughing. Neat rows of paired gloves seemed to line the entire trunk. "Oh!"

"Yep, welcome to my world," said Elsa.

"Wait," said Anna, reaching into the trunk. Something had caught her eye. It was a small, tattered toy that appeared to be worn from many years of love. Anna lifted the strange little creature out of the trunk. It was made of yarn and had one button eye, a cape, and a few straggly pieces of orange hair sticking out the top of its oddly shaped head. "Who's this little guy?"

Delighted, Elsa grabbed it. "Oh, Sir Jorgenborgen!" she exclaimed, giving it a big hug. She stared at it lovingly as she played with a strand of his yarn hair and sighed. "He was a really good listener."

She cradled him for a moment before looking at her sister. "Anna, how are we going to find any signs of traditions up here?" She didn't think being in the attic was going to solve their problem. Ready to give up and go back downstairs, she tossed Sir Jorgenborgen back into the trunk. But as he landed, she heard the faint ringing of bells. Her face brightened as the sound

sparked an old, dusty memory. She reached into her trunk, curious. "Unless . . . ," she said with a sly smile as she rummaged around. Suddenly, she lifted out a wooden box. A delicate design was carved into it, and tiny golden bells sat on top.

"What's that?" asked Anna.

"Look inside," said Elsa, holding the box out to her sister.

Anna paused for a moment, enjoying the suspense before slowly opening the mysterious box. She gasped, surprised to see what was inside. A smile crept across her face and she happily gazed up at her sister. They both knew what they had to do next. With the box in hand, they hurried down from the attic to find Olaf.

## Chapter 9

Out in the mountains, dusk was long gone. It was getting late. The stars began to twinkle and shine against the darkening blue sky. Olaf stood at the edge of the cliff and looked over at Sven, way on the other side of the deep canyon.

"Okay, Sven," he called. "I'm not going to sugarcoat it: this is a bit of a setback."

The reindeer stood and watched as Olaf looked at a few of the destroyed items that had fallen out of the sleigh around him.

"Oh. Maybe this is salvageable," Olaf said,

picking up a crown made of candles. He put it on his head and it crumbled apart. "No, definitely not." He spotted a holiday vase and picked it up. "Parts of this are still good, I think." The vase cracked and shards of glass dropped to the ground. "Oh no. This is unsafe now." He tried to move the broken pieces into a pile.

Refusing to give up hope, Olaf continued to scan the surrounding area, searching for one single item he could bring back to Elsa and Anna. He couldn't imagine that he might be left with nothing after all his hard work. His eyes lit up when he finally discovered something that was still fully intact.

"Hey!" he shouted. "The fruitcake!" He picked up the dense dessert. "These things are indestructible." He held it up to show Sven.

Olaf tried to figure out what to do next. He was happy to have found something to take to the castle, but how would he and Sven get back? He turned toward the thick, dark forest behind him and called out to Sven, "I'll just take this

seemingly harmless shortcut here and meet you back at the castle, okay?"

Sven could only watch helplessly as Olaf disappeared into the darkness.

Seconds later, a pack of wolves howled in the distance. Sven pawed at the snow, trying to find a way over the chasm. But he could only listen as he heard Olaf say, "Ohhh, puppies!" Then the wolves began to growl. "Down, boy," said Olaf. "Sit. Ah! I'm just gonna go— Noooo!" Olaf's scream faded into the forest.

Sven couldn't get to his friend. With no other choice, he raced back to the castle as fast as he could.

Meanwhile, a strange scent wafted through the stables as Kristoff finished making his traditional Flemmy Stew. Thoroughly enjoying the process, he hummed happily as he stirred the big pot. Feeling like a true chef, he reached out

and grabbed various items, and threw them into the pot between each stir. He smelled the steam coming off the stew and gave an approving nod.

Just then, like a bolt of lightning, Sven burst through the door. He was running so fast that he couldn't stop. He smashed right into the back wall!

"Sven!" said Kristoff excitedly. "The Flemmy Stew is ready!"

Sven breathlessly raced over to Kristoff.

"Anna and Elsa are gonna love this," Kristoff continued, unaware that Sven was trying to get his attention.

Sven nudged Kristoff, butting his head against his shoulder. He made a loud groaning noise, trying to tell Kristoff about Olaf, but Kristoff didn't seem to get it. Kristoff lowered his voice, pretending to speak for Sven. *"Oh, Kristoff, you're so thoughtful! Now, where's my bowl?"*

Frustrated, Sven ran toward his stall. Kristoff slipped back into his regular voice.

"Hey, simmer down, buddy. Here you go."

He brought Sven a big bowl of stew. Sven turned away, picked a carrot up with his mouth, and stuck it into the center of the bowl.

"Whoa," said Kristoff to Sven. "What are you—"

Sven pushed on the carrot with his hoof, trying to make it stick straight up. The stew now vaguely resembled Olaf's face, complete with his carrot nose.

"Oh," said Kristoff. "Of course!" Sven nodded enthusiastically, thrilled that Kristoff was finally picking up on his signals.

Kristoff slipped into his Sven voice. *Needs more carrots.* Sven grunted and frowned, surprised at how difficult it was to communicate with his best friend.

"Can't get enough of 'em, can ya?" asked Kristoff in his regular voice.

Irritated, Sven used his teeth to pull the carrot out of the bowl of stew. He would have to think of another way to explain. He grabbed a couple of sticks and tried to make himself look like Olaf,

using them as twig arms. He wobbled around, mimicking the little snowman.

Using some bales of hay, Sven attempted to act out the scary scene in the forest. He ducked behind the hay and howled like a wolf. Then he suddenly popped out, pretending to be Olaf. He sank behind the hay and came up again, this time showing his teeth, growling, and pretending to be a ferocious wolf. He continued to play the parts of Olaf and the wolves, hiding as he changed characters, trying to demonstrate what had happened. Kristoff watched, utterly puzzled by Sven's behavior.

"Uh," Kristoff said, clueless.

Neither Sven nor Kristoff had noticed Anna and Elsa standing in the doorway behind them. The sisters had not been able to find Olaf and had decided to check with Kristoff. They had witnessed Sven's entire performance.

"Oh no!" Anna said urgently. "Olaf is lost in the forest?"

"And being chased by hungry wolves?" added Elsa.

Relieved, Sven nodded. The sisters had understood him perfectly!

"Uh, yeah!" said Kristoff. "Obviously," he added, awkwardly clearing his throat. He set down the stew and hurried after Elsa and Anna as they ran out of the stables. A moment later he poked his head in and looked at Sven, who was finally catching his breath. "C'mon, Sven! Make yourself useful. Olaf needs our help!"

Sven grunted, following Kristoff. Outside in the darkness, the worried group worked on a plan to help find their lost friend.

# Chapter 10

The moon hung in the night sky, casting a dim glow on the dark forest below. With the wolves running behind him, Olaf bolted down a twisted path. He had never been in the forest alone at night before, and the darkness made it especially scary. Terrifying shadows appeared, and strange animal noises sounded and cackled from every corner. Olaf tried his best to shut it all out and focus only on his escape. He simply had to get that fruitcake back to Anna and Elsa.

The wolves charged after him, their yellow eyes narrowing as they ran faster and faster. Olaf

panted as he ran as fast as he could, clutching the fruitcake. He scraped past thorny branches, but they didn't slow him down. The angry wolves growled, snarled, and drooled as they continued to chase him, getting closer and closer.

"Please!" he shouted breathlessly. "I know you're hungry, but I need at least one item for my best friends." The wolves nipped at his heels. "The fate of the world depends on it!"

Olaf could see that the path ahead was blocked by thick, gnarled branches and brambles. He spotted a few small gaps in the brush and came up with a plan. In one swift move, he flung the fruitcake into one of the holes and then jumped through, splitting himself apart so he could fit.

Moments later, the disassembled snowman and the fruitcake were both safe on the other side. The wolves snapped and growled angrily as they tried to get to him, sticking their noses through and pawing at the ground. But they were too large to squeeze past the brambles. They whimpered as the thorns pricked into

their skin, until they finally gave up. With one final sigh, they turned and headed back down the path.

Relieved, Olaf put himself back together and took a deep breath. He had survived the chase, but he looked completely disheveled. One of his eyes was puffed up to the size of a small snowball, and he was covered from head to toe in scratches, bruises, dirt, and leaves. Even his nose had slid over to the back of his head. But he didn't care one bit. In fact, he felt great! Thrilled, he picked up the fruitcake and shouted, "Yes! I did it!" He danced a joyful jig around in the snow. "A tradition is saved!" He held the cake up, victorious.

*SCREECH! SCREECH!* Just then, a giant hawk gracefully swooped down and swiped the fruitcake from his grip! Olaf's smile sank as he watched the bird fly off, cawing as it carried the cake away in its thick talons. He stared up at the sky, astounded, until the bird disappeared into the dark night. He couldn't believe the only thing

he'd managed to save was gone. He had failed.

Deflated, Olaf sighed. "Well, I guess hawks need traditions, too," he said, pushing his nose back into place.

Olaf felt terrible. The last thing he wanted to do was let Elsa and Anna down. Slumped over, with his head hanging low, he slowly walked a few paces. He sunk down in the snow and collapsed against a tree. "Maybe I should just stay lost." He settled into his spot.

As the sad little snowman sat, feeling worse than he ever had before, the snow began to gently fall, and soon covered him like a blanket.

# Chapter 11

The Yule Bell rang out across the kingdom, alerting everyone that something was happening. Anna and Elsa knew that Olaf needed all the help they could get. Along with Kristoff, they knocked on doors, explaining what had happened as they gathered a search party.

Soon it seemed as if everyone in the kingdom had come together to help. Armed with lanterns, they headed into the mountains to look for Olaf.

When they got to the forest, the group split up, fanning out in different directions.

"Olaf! Olaf!" they called, searching every corner of the forest.

Elsa and Anna went off together, calling out his name as they hurried through the snow.

"He's not here," said a familiar voice. Elsa and Anna exchanged a relieved look, then rushed toward a carrot sticking out of a nearby snowdrift.

"Hmm, I wonder where he went," said Anna, smiling widely at Elsa.

"Well, he probably went on a mission to find traditions for Anna and Elsa," said Olaf's voice.

"Did he find any?" asked Elsa.

"He did, but they caught fire and fell off a cliff, and then they caught fire again," the voice said sadly.

Sven trotted over and sniffed the snow. He followed the scent trail all the way to the carrot. Using his teeth, he pulled Olaf out of the snowdrift by his nose.

"And then a hawk took them," Olaf added blankly. He looked up at the sisters and sighed.

"I'm sorry. You still don't have a tradition."

"But we do, Olaf. Look," said Anna. She knelt and held up the old wooden box from Elsa's trunk. Then she opened it and showed him its contents.

Olaf peered inside and gasped. His eyes brightened. "Wait. . . ." He reached toward the box. "Is that . . . ?" His voice cracked a little as it trailed off. He was speechless at the sight. Inside were dozens of drawings, paintings, and sculptures—and every one was of him!

"Anna made these years ago when we first created you," explained Elsa. "You were the one who brought us together and kept us connected when we were apart."

"Every Christmas, I made Elsa a gift," Anna said proudly.

She and Elsa shared their memory with Olaf and explained how each year, Anna would slip her homemade gift beneath Elsa's door. And even though they couldn't celebrate the holidays together, they both looked forward to their little tradition.

"All those long years alone," said Anna, "we had you to remind us of our childhood. Of how much we still loved each other."

"It's *you*, Olaf," said Elsa with a smile. "*You* are our tradition."

"Me?" said Olaf, touched.

"Surprise," said Anna with a quiet chuckle.

The sisters leaned in and gave the little snowman a great big warm hug.

"Oohhh," said Olaf. His heart was nearly bursting with joy.

In that moment, the three realized that being together was the best thing they could ever wish for during the holidays. They had no need for anything else when they had each other!

Elsa waved her arms and a bow tie made of ice appeared around Olaf's neck to replace his missing flower petal. He smiled and thanked her, appreciating the fancy touch.

Soon all the townspeople ran over, thrilled that the sisters had found Olaf. Ben, who had given Olaf a candy cane just hours before, was at the front of the group. A huge smile spread

across his face when he saw that the snowman was safe.

"Olaf!" he exclaimed, running up to him. "We were worried about you." He handed Olaf one of his homemade candy canes.

A bunch of the other children ran to Olaf. They all held hands and danced around him in the snow, celebrating his safety.

Just then, Elsa had an amazing idea: they could have the party with everyone out there in the woods! She waved her arms and created a beautiful little ice fence, lining a pathway for Olaf and his friends to run down. Then she waved her arms again and made an ice-skating rink!

Elsa grabbed Anna's hand, and they began to skate and dance happily across the rink. They pulled Kristoff and Olaf onto the ice, and soon everyone joined in, skating and having a great time. Even Oaken skated by, wearing another tiny towel! He was very graceful, and he jumped into the air on his skates, spun around, and landed perfectly, impressing everyone.

The servants brought out all the trays of food from the castle and set them on ornate ice tables that Elsa had created. Olaf shared some hot cocoa with a group of kids. Everyone was so happy to be together.

Elsa couldn't help adding another magical touch to the wonderful occasion. She stomped her foot, sending her magic through the ground. Suddenly, an ice tree sprang up and continued to grow and grow, towering in the night sky. It sparkled in the starlight, looking absolutely stunning.

Elsa waved her arms and lanterns magically floated up, decorating the beautiful ice tree.

Anna removed a little straw Olaf sculpture from the old wooden box and held it out to Elsa, who encased it in a star made of ice. Then she used her magic to float Olaf to the upper boughs of the tree. The snowman set the beautiful ice star at the very top. Elsa helped Olaf down, and then he landed on Sven's head and sat comfortably between his antlers.

Once the tree was complete, everyone took a moment to admire it. They gazed up at its beauty, appreciating being together.

"Well," said Elsa, kneeling beside Olaf. "I think Arendelle has a new tradition."

"Thank you, Olaf," said Anna, joining her sister.

With Elsa and Anna on either side of him, Olaf knew he was the luckiest snowman in the world. With the moonlight's reflection on the ice and the lanterns glowing against the tree, they were all perfectly happy. Everyone had gotten a surprise that holiday. It was their first—and best—winter together.

*THUMP!* Just then, the stolen fruitcake fell from the sky and landed on Olaf's head, driving him into the snow.

"The fruitcake!" he mumbled happily. "It's a Christmas miracle!"